DATE DUE

Home

A JOURNEY THROUGH AMERICA

ILLUSTRATED BY

Thomas Locker

EDITED BY THOMAS LOCKER AND CANDACE CHRISTIANSEN

Silver Whistle

Harcourt Brace & Company

SAN DIEGO   NEW YORK   LONDON

To Miriam Suzanne

Requests for permission to make copies of any part of the work should be mailed to: Permissions Department, Harcourt Brace & Company, 6277 Sea Harbor Drive, Orlando, Florida 32887-6777.

"Once by the Pacific" from THE POETRY OF ROBERT FROST EDITED BY EDWARD CONNERY LATHEM, © 1956 by Robert Frost, Copyright 1928, © 1969 by Henry Holt and Company, Inc. Reprinted by permission of Henry Holt and Company, Inc. "Gold" copyright © 1998 by Pat Mora. Excerpt from "Fog" in CHICAGO POEMS, copyright 1916 by Holt, Rinehart and Winston, Inc. and renewed 1944 by Carl Sandburg, reprinted by permission of Harcourt Brace & Company. "The River" copyright © 1998 by Jane Yolen reprinted by permission of Curtis Brown, Ltd. "Children of the Sky" copyright © 1998 by Joseph Bruchac. "Tree" copyright © 1998 by Eloise Greenfield. From "Song of a People" by Merle Good, copyright © 1993 by Good Books. Reprinted by permission of Good Books. "Birches in the Fall" copyright © 1998 by Thomas Locker.

Silver Whistle is a registered trademark of Harcourt Brace & Company.

Library of Congress Cataloging-in-Publication Data
Home: a journey through America/[compiled and illustrated by] Thomas Locker.
p. cm.
"Silver Whistle."
Summary: An anthology of poetry and prose by such writers as Carl Sandburg, Willa Cather, and Robert Frost, all celebrating aspects of the American landscape.
ISBN 0-15-201473-X
1. Landscape—United States—Literary collections. 2. Children's literature, American.
[1. Landscape—Literary collections] I. Locker, Thomas, 1937—
PZ5.H749 1998
810.8'032—dc21 97-18206

PRINTED IN HONG KONG GFEDCB

Introduction

HOME is more than just the place we return to after being away. Home is something that becomes part of us as we live in it. For artists and writers, home can become part of how we see the world and how we shape our words or our artwork. For everyone, the place we call home becomes a part of our lives.

For the past ten years I have lived in the Hudson River valley of New York. I can see the river and the Catskill Mountains from my studio, and I often go out on foot with my easel and paint box to see trails and cliffs and waterfalls. Most of my paintings are landscapes—what other artists consider background is the focus of my work, and my favorite subject is the Hudson River valley—my home.

For *Home: A Journey through America*, Candace Christiansen and I have selected writings and commissioned poems from writers with individual and personal ways of seeing and describing the landscape where they make their homes. From the seacoasts to the plains to the desert, this collection of poems, prose, and blessings defines what home is to many of us. I have had the pleasure of creating artwork for these words. It is my hope that this book will present a vision of our varied and special land, and that *Home* will inspire readers to celebrate the special places they call home.

—T. L.

From *Once by the Pacific*

ROBERT FROST

The shattered water made a misty din.
Great waves looked over others coming in,
And thought of doing something to the shore
That water never did to land before.
The clouds were low and hairy in the skies,
Like locks blown forward in the gleam of eyes.
You could not tell, and yet it looked as if
The shore was lucky in being backed by cliff,
The cliff in being backed by continent. . . .

Robert Frost was born in San Francisco and lived in
California as a child, before moving to New England,
where he lived most of his life. He is one of America's
most beloved poets.

Children of the Sky

JOSEPH BRUCHAC

Winds whisper
across the Comanche prairie,
A breathless chant
between promise and prayer.

We are alive
    we are alive.

Bluebonnets answer,
bowing their heads
toward the billowing clouds,
the slow song of the sky.

We are alive,
    we are alive.

White birds of power
soon will open their wings
bring rain to thirsty earth again,
sweet as the sight of home
to a traveler's eye.

We are alive,
    we are alive,
        we are all
            the children of the sky.

Joseph Bruchac, a poet and storyteller, wrote this poem after traveling through the area of Texas that is the home of the Comanche Indian people. The poem is based on their traditional understanding of that place, the land, the plants, and earth and sky.

Tree

ELOISE GREENFIELD

Tree stands on storied ground,
like its brothers and sisters
in cities and towns.
listens. hears life.
weaves voices in its limbs.

cascades songs and tears and laughter,
new and old sounds overlapping.
Tree stands on storied ground,
rippling its leaves to the rhythms
of home.

*Eloise Greenfield, poet and author, was born in Parmele,
North Carolina. There she lived on a tree-lined street,
as she does today in Washington, D.C.*

My Childhood's Home

ABRAHAM LINCOLN

My childhood's home I see again,
    And sadden with the view;
And still, as memory crowds my brain,
    There's pleasure in it too.
O Memory! thou midway world
    'Twixt earth and paradise,

Where things decayed and loved ones lost
    In dreamy shadows rise,
And, freed from all that's earthly vile,
    Seem hallowed, pure, and bright,
Like scenes in some enchanted isle
    All bathed in liquid light. . . .

Abraham Lincoln was president of the United States during the Civil War. His speeches and essays, including the Gettysburg Address, Thanksgiving Proclamation, and Emancipation Proclamation, represent some of the finest writings of that time. Abraham Lincoln's childhood home was in Spencer County, Indiana.

From the *Journal*

HENRY DAVID THOREAU

Every day a new picture is painted and framed, held up for half an hour,
in such lights as the Great Artist chooses, and then withdrawn,
and the curtain falls.
And then the sun goes down, and long the afterglow gives light.
And then the damask curtains glow along the western window.
And now the first star is lit, and I go home.

Henry David Thoreau is considered one of the first
environmentalists. He lived in a cabin he built on the
shore of Walden Pond, near Concord, Massachusetts,
and wrote this passage on January 7, 1852.

PACIFIC
OCEAN

AK

WA

OR

ID

MT

ND

MN

SD

NV

WY

NE

RED CLOUD
Cather's
My Ántonia

IA

MO

SAN FRANCISCO
Frost's
"Once by the Pacific"

UT

CO

KS

YOSEMITE FALLS
Muir's
"Climb the Mountains"

CA

AZ

SANTA FE
Mora's *"Gold"*

NM

OK

AR

HI

NORTHERN TEXAS
Bruchac's
"Children of the Sky"

TX

N
W   E
S

LAKE SUPERIOR

LAKE HURON

LAKE MICHIGAN

LAKE ONTARIO

LAKE ERIE

WI

MI

IN

IL

OH

KY

TN

MS

AL

LA

GA

FL

NC

SC

VA

WV

MD

DC

DE

NJ

PA

NY

VT

ME

NH

MA

CT

RI

CHICAGO
Sandburg's "Fog"

SPENCER COUNTY
Lincoln's "My Childhood's Home"

LANCASTER
Good's "Song of a People"

HUDSON RIVER VALLEY
Irving's *Rip Van Winkle*

WALDEN POND
Thoreau's Journal

HATFIELD, MA
Yolen's "The River"

WASHINGTON, CT
Locker's "Birches in the Fall"

PARMELE, NC
Greenfield's "Tree"

ATLANTIC OCEAN

GULF OF MEXICO

WRITERS in this BOOK

Joseph Bruchac, born 1942
Saratoga Springs, NY

Willa Cather, born 1873
Winchester, VA

Robert Frost, born 1874
San Francisco, CA

Merle Good, born 1946
Lititz, PA

Eloise Greenfield, born 1929
Parmele, NC

Washington Irving, born 1783
New York, NY

Abraham Lincoln, born 1809
Larue County, KY

Thomas Locker, born 1937
New York, NY

Pat Mora, born 1942
El Paso, TX

John Muir, born 1838
Dunbar, Scotland

Carl Sandburg, born 1878
Galesburg, IL

Henry David Thoreau, born 1817
Concord, MA

Jane Yolen, born 1939
New York, NY

The illustrations in this book were done in oils on canvas.
The text type was set in Goudy Village.
The display type was hand lettered by Georgia Deaver.
Map by Georgia Deaver
Color separations by Bright Arts, Ltd., Hong Kong
Printed by South China Printing Company, Ltd., Hong Kong
This book was printed on totally chlorine-free Nymolla Matte Art paper.
Production supervision by Stanley Redfern and Ginger Boyer
Designed by Michael and Ryan Farmer